THE 3·2·3 DETECTIVE AGENCY

in

The Disappearance of Dave Warthog

FIONA ROBINSON

AMULET BOOKS
New York

THEY MET ON THE 3:23 P.M. TRAIN TO WHISKA CITY. THEY STARTED OFF AS STRANGERS BUT QUICKLY FOUND SOMETHING IN COMMON. EACH WANTED TO START A NEW LIFE IN THE BIG CITY...

ROGER THE DUNG BEETLE TOLD HIS STORY FIRST...

MEANWHILE, IN NEARBY SLOTH WOODS ...

Did something happen today?

I think Slingshot went to the city.

Cool ... zzz

BACK ON THE 3-2-3 EXPRESS, PRISCILLA, A PENGUIN, SPOKE NEXT ...

LADIES AND GENTLEMEN!

My dream ... since I was an egg ... has been TO ACT! It is in Whiska City that I will SHINE like a STAR!

SHE BOWED. EVERYONE CLAPPED, WITHOUT QUITE KNOWING WHY...

This is my swan!

S-T-R-E-T-C-H

And this ... is my eagle!

FROM THE CORNER OF THE COMPARTMENT, THEY HEARD A SMALL SCREAM ...

AAAARGH!

IT WAS BLUEBELL THE RAT ...

Oh ... you're very good! Phew! I really thought you might eat me!

Priscilla, which play will you star in First, so we can see you?

Erm ... I don't have a role yet. I may have to get a different kind of job until I get my First big break.

Erm, erm ... well my story ISN'T exciting like everyone else's. I'm just a country rat. I knit and make plum jelly.

One day I woke up and thought, "I wish I could do something *really* interesting and make new friends ..." I hope Whiska City will open my eyes ... but I also hope it won't be scary!

Oh ... maybe I'll get off this train right away!

NO!

I'll look after you. Stick with me!

THERE WAS ONE TRAVELER LEFT TO SPEAK. SHE WAS JENNY, A DONKEY ...

I'm going to Whiska City to set up a detective agency!

What's that?

Well, if someone needs something investigated and the police can't help, then my agency would look into it. Here's an example: someone very mean has stolen your garden gnome ...

Oh my, that's very, very naughty!

But I haven't got a garden gnome!

We're just pretending. The police are busy with a bank robbery. And you want your gnome now! So you hire a private detective, like me, to find it.

PRISCILLA STARTED TO ACT ...

OH, POOR little gnomie. I love him so much!

I've saved up enough money to start the business. Now I need talented folk like you to work with me as detectives!

US?

YOU!

5

CHAPTER TWO

AS THE 3:23 P.M. TRAIN SPED ALONG,
THE NEW FRIENDS CHATTED ...

But Jenny, what will I *do* in your detective agency?

You're very energetic, Slingshot. You'd be great at chasing down suspects!

Hey! Come back with that garden gnome!

But I'm an actress! I haven't got ANY detective skills ...

You'd be excellent at going undercover, Priscilla!

What's "going undercover"?

It's when you pretend to be someone else to get closer to the criminal!

Imagine someone has been stealing Fruit from a grocery store ...

That's *really* naughty!

Is it the same suspect who stole the garden gnome?

Remember, we're just pretending! To go undercover, Priscilla would get a job at the store, acting as a clerk. She'd watch for anything suspicious.

Plastic or paper bags, sir?

Paper, please, miss!

PEARS

POTATOES

Could ... could I be of any use?

Yes, Bluebell! You would be superb at surveillance! You're well camouflaged and, erm, smallish.

Surveillance? You mean watching a suspect to see what they're up to ...

Yeah, I got the money! You got the goods?

Well, I doubt you can find something for a chef to do! The only crime I've ever come across is lumpy mashed potatoes!

Roger, we'll need to eat. You could be our chef! PLUS ... your fine gourmet nose could be one of the best detecting devices we have!

Superb!

AND JENNY WAS DAYDREAMING, TOO ...

Certificate OF BRILLIANCE

BEST DETECTIVE AGENCY

EVERYONE SHOOK PAWS OR HOOVES OR LEGS OR FLIPPERS ...

Hey, let's call ourselves the 3-2-3 Detective Agency, so we'll always remember that we met on the 3-2-3 train!

YEAH!

JUST THEN THE CONDUCTOR CAME IN ...

Tickets, please! So you're all for Whiska City? Word of advice, STICK TOGETHER! Lots of folks have gone missing ... No one knows why!

CHAPTER THREE

THE 3:23 P.M. TRAIN PULLED INTO WHISKA CITY. IT WAS RUSH HOUR, AND BUSINESS ANIMALS DASHED IN ALL DIRECTIONS. SLINGSHOT SCOOPED UP BLUEBELL AND ROGER SO THEY WOULDN'T GET LOST ...

THE FRIENDS WENT DOWN TO THE SUBWAY ...

PINK PERFECTOR POODLES HAIRDRESSERS OF THE YEAR!

ALL TRAINS STOP AT TERMITE HEIGHTS

AND TOOK A TRAIN TO TERMITE HEIGHTS, WHERE JENNY HAD RENTED AN OFFICE ...

250 YEARS OF EXPERIENCE! TURTLELAW. COM

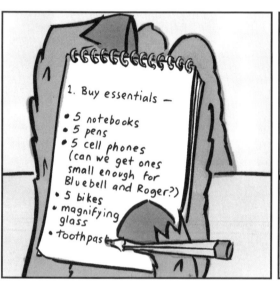

ON THE NEXT PAGE, SHE WROTE ...

JENNY LOOKED AT HER NEW FRIENDS.
SUDDENLY, SHE WAS WORRIED ...

Oh boy, I hope they'll never HAVE to defend themselves!

THE SUBWAY TRAIN PULLED INTO TERMITE HEIGHTS. IT SEEMED LIKE AN UNFRIENDLY PLACE ...

Erm, Jenny, have you got the right address?

Yes. It should be just around this corner ... Number 8 Platypus Place.

WOW!

PLATYPUS PLACE WAS FULL OF LIFE! THERE WAS AN OUTDOOR CAFE WITH A BAND PLAYING ...

Table for five, guys?

Doot doot, 'n' doobie doot! Doobie doot 'n' doobie doo ... YEAH!

Sure!

SOON THEY WERE SIPPING THEIR DRINKS ...

Hey! Look at this sign!

TOOTS TURTLE WILL NOT PERFORM TONIGHT, DUE TO HIS MYSTERIOUS DISAPPEARANCE. "THE NEWTS" WILL APPEAR INSTEAD.

Oh my!

That's strange! Let's ask our waiter about Toots Turtle! Every detective must be inquisitive! Let's start now!

THEIR WAITER, CHASE FERRET, WAS HAPPY TO CHAT ...

Yes, it's odd about Toots. His wife, Lulu, called earlier today to say she couldn't find him! He went out on some errands and didn't come back. I hope he's OK!

So do we!

JENNY PAID THE CHECK. THEY WALKED DOWN THE STREET ...

KEEPING EVEN CLOSER TOGETHER THAN BEFORE ...

THEY ARRIVED AT NUMBER 8, THEIR NEW HOME ...

CHAPTER FOUR

NUMBER 8 PLATYPUS PLACE WAS OWNED BY BROCK BADGER, THEIR NEW LANDLORD. IT HAD A GOURMET COFFEE STORE ON THE FIRST FLOOR …

Am I in heaven?

No, son, but if you're the new renters, you've come to the right place! Name's Brock! Pleased to meet you!

BROCK SHOOK THEIR HANDS …

Boy, he has a strong grip!

Wha …?

OK, Jen, breathe deeply and think of cute puppies!

AARRGH! I'll never knit again!

I'm Roger!

Son, you have a firm handshake, and I like that in an insect!

BROCK SHOWED THEM IN ...

You'll be on the second floor ...

BEST COFFEE

I furnished it as per your instructions, Jenny!

Well, whadd'ya think?

Brock, it's perfect!

COOL!

Good. I'll let you settle in.

I think we should each find a place to sleep now. Tomorrow we'll explore the city and start detective training!

ROGER WENT TO THE KITCHEN. HE QUICKLY FOUND AN EGG CUP TO REST IN ...

PRISCILLA WADDLED INTO THE BATHROOM ...

Could someone be a darling and get me some ice?

Lovely! Thank you, sweetheart.

BLUEBELL SNUGGLED UNDER A PLANT ...

HOME SWEET HOME

SLINGSHOT SETTLED ON THE COATRACK. THE SLOTH WHO NEVER SLEEPS FELL ASLEEP AT ONCE ...

BUT JENNY LAY AWAKE FOR A WHILE, STILL EXCITED FROM THE DAY'S EVENTS ...

HER DREAM OF RUNNING A DETECTIVE AGENCY WAS FINALLY HAPPENING. AND SHE HAD MADE NEW FRIENDS, TOO!

CHAPTER FIVE

THE NEXT DAY, JENNY WOKE UP WITH A DUNG BEETLE ON HER NOSE...

... and the muffins will be another two minutes. I'm thinking raspberry preserves and butter with them! But let's start with scrambled eggs. I've been up since six A.M. Thank you for this great job, Jenny. It's so exciting!

Roger, what are you talking about?

Oh ... BREAKFAST IS SERVED!

AS THE FRIENDS ATE, JENNY OUTLINED HER PLAN FOR THE DAY...

I think we should buy bicycles first, so we can get around the city easily. There's a store nearby, Bella Gorilla's Bicycle Bonanza.

• HALIBUT WAY •

Hi!

Howdy!

Morning!

Hello!

Hi!

Morning!

Hi!

TOADS
FURNITUR
AMPHIBI

HOP
IN!

THEY FOUND THE BIKE STORE ...

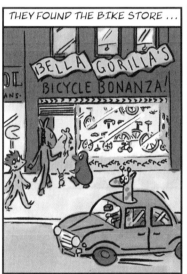

BELLA GORILLA'S
BICYCLE BONANZA!

BUT BELLA, THE OWNER, WASN'T AROUND ...

TIRES
SURE
FOOT
by GOAT

ELEPHA ⟨⟨RAC

Boy, these bikes are
expensive. We'll have to
see if Bella has any
special offers.

$100.00

A GORILLA APPEARED ...

I can help. I dunno where my
lazy lump of a daughter is. She
left yesterday to get her legs
waxed. Well, those beauticians
must be very thorough!
Anyway ... what d'ya want?

You're mean!
Maybe something awful
has happened to your
daughter!

THUMP

Oh, my poor darling girl! I bet you're right! She's gone, GONE! I didn't mean to sound so nasty. I love her, really!

JENNY COMFORTED HIM ...

I'm sure Bella's OK. She is a fully grown gorilla, after all!

SHE GLARED AT SLINGSHOT ...

I'm sorry, I'm sorry! I should think before I speak!

Mr. Gorilla, we're private detectives. We'll keep a lookout for Bella. But can you help us, too? We need bikes to get around town, but we don't have much money.

I have just the thing!

MR. GORILLA LEAPT UP ...

This was ordered by five circus clowns, but they never picked it up. Huh, very funny! Anyway ... if you find my beautiful Bella, you can have it.

18

Hmmm ... now what does this do?

Er, thank you ... We'll take it. And we'll try our very best to find Bella!

NEXT THEY PICKED OUT SAFETY HELMETS ...

Safe AND stylish!

19

TEN MINUTES LATER ...

Great! This ... will get us ... around town ... and keep us all ... very fit ...! Phew!

Oh, sure it'll keep us fit!

I'm feeling slimmer already!

Me too!

Me three!

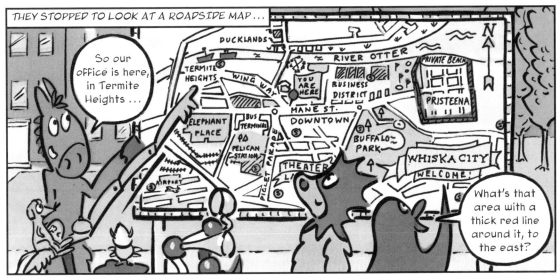

THEY STOPPED TO LOOK AT A ROADSIDE MAP ...

So our office is here, in Termite Heights ...

What's that area with a thick red line around it, to the east?

DUCKLANDS
RIVER OTTER
PRIVATE BEACH
TERMITE HEIGHTS
WING WAY
YOU ARE HERE
BUSINESS DISTRICT
PRISTEENA
MANE ST.
DOWNTOWN
ELEPHANT PLACE
BUS TERMINAL
PELICAN STATION
PIGLET PARADE
BUFFALO PARK
WHISKA CITY WELCOME!
THEATER LA
AIRPORT
N

PRIVATE BEACH
PRISTEENA
N

Oh, look at that! It's that community designed just for poodles! Pristeena. I read about it on the subway. Does anyone want to check it out?

Nah! Sounds boring!

FOR TWO HOURS, THEY CYCLED AROUND THE CITY ...

THEN JENNY REALIZED ...

THROB THROB

SHE WAS DOING ...

ALL THE PEDALING ...

SO THE FRIENDS WENT TO BUFFALO PARK, WHERE JENNY SOAKED HER ACHING HOOVES IN THE LAKE ...

I wish someone had told me!

NEAR THE LAKE, THEY STOPPED TO ADMIRE A STATUE ...

ROARINGTON WHISKA

SHIPPING MAGNATE & FOUNDER OF WHISKA CITY

"I BELIEVE THAT ALL CITIZENS OF WHISKA CITY, BE THEY SCALED, PLUMED, OR JUST PLAIN FURRY, ARE BORN EQUAL. A MOOSE AND A MOUSE SHALL BOTH WALK TALL HERE. THROUGH FRIENDSHIP OUR CITY WILL BE THE GREATEST IN THE WORLD."

So he was a shipping magnate? That means he was stuck to the side of a boat, right? Like a refrigerator magnate, but way bigger.

Erm, no. You are thinking of a magnet. He was a magnate. It means he owned a fleet of ships. Roarington Whiska used the harbor here as his base, and created jobs for the first settlers.

Oh ... right ... Can we go shopping now?

THEY FOUND A STORE THAT CLAIMED TO SELL EVERYTHING ...

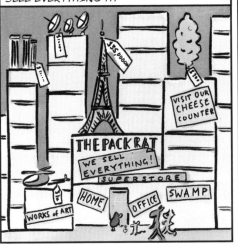

THE PACK RAT
WE SELL EVERYTHING!
SUPERSTORE
HOME   OFFICE   SWAMP
WORKS OF ART
VISIT OUR CHEESE COUNTER

INSIDE, FRANTIC-LOOKING RATS SCURRIED AROUND HELPING THE CUSTOMERS ...

AISLE 53
BOTTLETOPS · ARTICHOKES · LE FRIZZ HAIR PRODUCTS · BALL GOWNS · MAGNIFYING GLASSES
STRING   ARTICHOKES   BALL GOWNS

Do you have this orange in red?

I'll check ...

JENNY FOUND SOMETHING FROM HER SHOPPING LIST ...

A magnifying glass can find tiny clues! It's very useful.

Oooh, Roger! You have lovely green eyes!

Why, thank you!

Aaaargh! Put it away! My feet look enormous!

CHAPTER SIX

THE FRIENDS SPENT THE AFTERNOON LEARNING DETECTIVE SKILLS. FIRST, JENNY TAUGHT THEM HOW TO BEHAVE WITH CLIENTS. PRISCILLA PRETENDED TO BE A CLIENT...

Oh, woe is me!

What's up? You look awful!

Let's try again! Slingshot...

Can you be a little more, erm... sensitive?

THEN THEY LEARNED HOW TO LOOK FOR CLUES ...

AHA!

So it was YOU who ate the last chocolate-chip cookie! I can see tiny crumbs on your nose! I'll go make some more!

THEY LEARNED HOW TO FOLLOW A SUSPECT WITHOUT BEING SEEN ...

1, 2, 3 ... I'm turning around, ready or not!

OH!

THEN THEY PRACTICED CONFRONTING A VILLAIN. PRISCILLA PRETENDED TO BE A TOUGH CROOK ...

You have been very naughty. I'm going to tell your mommy!

Oh yeah? See if I care, shorty!

We'll practice again later. Don't worry, you're doing very well!

26

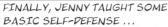
FINALLY, JENNY TAUGHT SOME BASIC SELF-DEFENSE ...

OK, guys, split into pairs. One of you attack, the other DEFEND!

AT THE END OF THE DAY, JENNY MADE A SHORT SPEECH ...

THEN SHE ASKED BLUEBELL TO PAINT THE AGENCY NAME ON THE OFFICE DOOR ...

IT GAVE THEM SOME WELL-EARNED CONFIDENCE.

CHAPTER SEVEN

THE NEXT MONDAY, THE DETECTIVES RAN AN
AD IN THE NEWSPAPER ...

Thanks ... Look, my best mate, Dave Warthog, is missing! We were supposed to go to the game last night, but he didn't show up!

He's not at home. He's not at work ... WHERE IS HE?

HE PAUSED AND SNIFFED ...

Do I smell cherry muffins?

Fresh from the oven. Help yourselves!

Great!

Cheers, Roger!

Yum, Roger!

JENNY SIGHED ...

Oh boy! My team is distracted already!

OK, guys! LET'S FOCUS! So Don, tell us more about Dave ...

Well, Dave's a regular guy like me, I guess. I went to his place to see if he was sick, but he's not there ...

Erm, excuse me! Maybe it would be good if someone went to Dave's place to look for clues. Maybe he's on vacation and forgot about his plans with Don. We could see if his suitcase is gone ... It's just an idea ...

Excellent, Bluebell! Go with Don now. Remember to take notes!

SO BLUEBELL WAS THE FIRST TO GO OUT AND INVESTIGATE! SHE SCUTTLED OVER TO DON. DON WAS SURPRISED. HE HADN'T NOTICED HER BEFORE ...

AFTER THEY LEFT, ANOTHER CLIENT ARRIVED. HER NAME WAS LEONA LIONESS ...

My husband, Lionel, has disappeared! He left for work and didn't come home!

When was this?

Yesterday ... I thought he was working late, but when I woke this morning, he STILL hadn't come home. So I called the police. They're not even answering the phone!

WE'LL find him!

Maybe he's been KIDNAPPED for a HUGE ransom! You're obviously wealthy, so that would make sense!

Did Slingshot really just say that?

I hadn't even thought he might have been kidnapped! WAAAAARGH!

OOOPS!

I'm sorry, I'm sorry. I should think before I speak!

One of my detectives will escort you home, Leona, and check Lionel's calendar.

Priscilla can see if he went to meet someone yesterday.

LEONA AND PRISCILLA LEFT ...

JUST THEN, DIGBY MUSKRAT, THEIR THIRD CLIENT, WADDLED IN ...

I'm worried about my mom!

She lives down the street from me and always brings me a big cake on Tuesday mornings ... until today! And her house is locked! I went to the police station for help. No one was there! I need to get inside. Mom could be hurt!

BEFORE JENNY COULD SPEAK ...

*

SLINGSHOT LEAPT IN ...

I can get in, EASILY! I can climb her house and jump down the chimney!

Let's go rescue Mom, Digby! ... Is that OK, Jenny?

Absolutely! Good idea, Slingshot!

SO DIGBY AND SLINGSHOT LEFT. ONLY JENNY AND ROGER REMAINED ...

Oh, Roger, so many animals in Whiska City have DISAPPEARED! I don't want one of us to disappear, too!

It's scary. And where are the police?

AT THAT MOMENT, THE MAYOR, WHO HAPPENED TO BE A MARE, RUSHED IN ...

IT'S AWFUL!

No one came to the Police Ball last night. I was there alone in a big stupid dress!

The entire police department has VANISHED!

So there's no police to investigate the disappearance of the police!

But there IS the 3-2-3 Detective Agency! I'll go to the station NOW and start the investigation!

JENNY GALLOPED OFF ...

NOW ONLY ROGER AND MAYOR MARE REMAINED ...

Oooh, I feel faint!

Oh boy!

Would you care for a muffin?

Thank you, dear!

CHAPTER EIGHT

BLUEBELL AND DON ARRIVED AT DAVE WARTHOG'S APARTMENT. INSIDE WAS A STRONG SMELL OF AFTERSHAVE ...

Wow! He only wears aftershave when he's meeting a lady! Maybe THAT'S where he is now!

That's interesting. I'll write it down. It may be a clue!

BLUEBELL SCUTTLED INTO THE BEDROOM. IT WAS A PIGSTY ...

His suitcase is under the bed. Yeuch! With a few old pizza boxes! So he wasn't planning to go away!

THEN SHE SEARCHED THE LIVING ROOM ...

Hmmmm ... what's this?

PRISCILLA FLIPPED THROUGH LIONEL'S DESK DIARY ...

Hmmm ... what does "MC" mean?

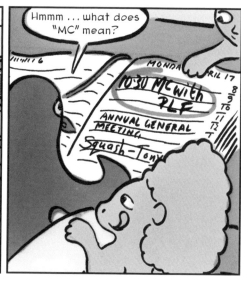

MONDAY APRIL 17
10:30 MC with PLF
ANNUAL GENERAL MEETING
Squash-Tony

JUST THEN, LEONA RETURNED ...

Here's his photo. You can take it back to the agency.

WOW! Erm, I mean ... I'm sorry ... but your husband has VERY BIG HAIR!

SUDDENLY, PRISCILLA HAD A PECULIAR FEELING ...

YIKES!

HA!

YEOOW!

CUBS, OUT! Where was I? Oh yes, Lionel does have big hair. He's a little ashamed of it. He was about to try the Mane Cure at Pootles Le Frizz's New You salon!

MANE CURE? That's what "MC" stands for! So "PLF" stands for "POOTLES LE FRIZZ"!

You see his ads all over town. I think this is a clue!

THEN SHE SMILED AT LEONA, FROWNED AT THE CUBS, AND WADDLED BACK TO THE AGENCY.

MEANWHILE, SLINGSHOT AND DIGBY ARRIVED AT DIGBY'S MOTHER'S HOME ...

Whoa ... stop! We're there!

SLINGSHOT LOOKED UP AT THE ROOF. THERE WAS NO CHIMNEY ...

I thought you wouldn't come if I said there was no chimney to jump down!

No problem! That open window will do!

Hmmmm! I wonder if that's the window to the bathr ...

SPLASH!

... oom! OOOPS!

TEN SECONDS LATER ...

Well, she's not in the toilet!

THEY QUICKLY SEARCHED THE HOUSE ...

Mom, are you in here?

THEY COULDN'T FIND DIGBY'S MOM ANYWHERE!

BREAD

37

A PORTRAIT OF DIGBY AND HIS MOM CAUGHT SLINGSHOT'S EYE ...

DIGBY STARTED TO CRY. SLINGSHOT WAS QUIET, FOR ONCE ...

IT STARTED TO RAIN. DIGBY DASHED TO THE WINDOW ...

Oh no! Mom's left her laundry out, too!

So Mom's MISSING!

Looks like it, Digby.

Ooooh!

A FACE APPEARED OVER THE HEDGE. IT WAS MRS. SLOW-LORIS, A NEIGHBOR ...

Ooooh! Did I hear you say Odora's missing? And I was chatting with her, right here, by THIS fence, yesterday! One minute she was talking about getting a curly perm, the next she's vanished. Ooooh!

A curly perm, you say ...? Digby, that may be a clue!

We'll start work on the case right away!

THEN HE GAVE DIGBY A HUG AND SPRINTED BACK TO THE AGENCY.

MEANWHILE, JENNY WAS AT THE POLICE STATION. IT WAS ABANDONED ...

Brrr! It's cold ... That door's been open all night.

Hmmm ... half-eaten chocolate cake. That's strange!

A PILE OF NEWSPAPERS FLUTTERED. JENNY JUMPED ...

AAAARRGHH!

SHE THOUGHT SOMEONE ELSE WAS THERE, BUT SHE SAW NO ONE ...

OK, Jen, be calm!

SHE WENT OVER TO THE PILE ...

Something's been cut out of all the newspapers! ...

THE HOLES WERE NEXT TO THE 3-2-3 AD ...

JENNY TRIED TO REMEMBER WHAT THE AD WAS FOR ...

HAD IT REALLY MADE THE ENTIRE POLICE DEPARTMENT DESERT THEIR DESSERT?

CHAPTER NINE

WHEN BLUEBELL, PRISCILLA, SLINGSHOT, AND JENNY RETURNED TO THE AGENCY, THEY FOUND ROGER CRYING. WHILE HE HAD BEEN OUT SHOPPING, THE OFFICE HAD BEEN RANSACKED!

Maybe someone's trying to scare us because *they're* scared of us!

Whoever did this must be connected with the disappearances! They want to frighten us because we're close to solving the crimes!

Let's clean up. Then we'll go over EVERYTHING we've learned today.

AS THEY WERE CLEANING, ROGER FOUND A BOBBY PIN. WAS IT ANOTHER CLUE?

THAT EVENING, THEY DISCUSSED THE CASES. AS THE DETECTIVES READ ALOUD THEIR NOTES, JENNY COPIED THEM ONTO THE CHALKBOARD ...

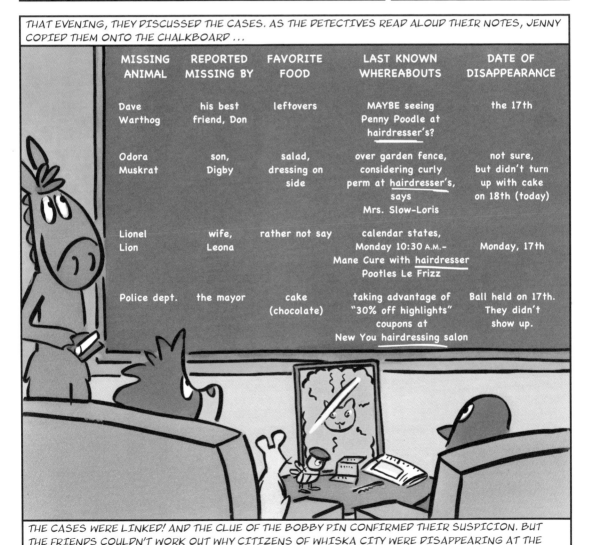

MISSING ANIMAL	REPORTED MISSING BY	FAVORITE FOOD	LAST KNOWN WHEREABOUTS	DATE OF DISAPPEARANCE
Dave Warthog	his best friend, Don	leftovers	MAYBE seeing Penny Poodle at hairdresser's?	the 17th
Odora Muskrat	son, Digby	salad, dressing on side	over garden fence, considering curly perm at hairdresser's, says Mrs. Slow-Loris	not sure, but didn't turn up with cake on 18th (today)
Lionel Lion	wife, Leona	rather not say	calendar states, Monday 10:30 A.M.– Mane Cure with hairdresser Pootles Le Frizz	Monday, 17th
Police dept.	the mayor	cake (chocolate)	taking advantage of "30% off highlights" coupons at New You hairdressing salon	Ball held on 17th. They didn't show up.

THE CASES WERE LINKED! AND THE CLUE OF THE BOBBY PIN CONFIRMED THEIR SUSPICION. BUT THE FRIENDS COULDN'T WORK OUT WHY CITIZENS OF WHISKA CITY WERE DISAPPEARING AT THE HAIRDRESSER'S! THE DETECTIVES MADE A PLAN FOR THE NEXT DAY ...

PRISCILLA PREPARED TO GO UNDERCOVER ...

Oh, darlings, how I have suffered!

SLINGSHOT PUT TOGETHER A COUPLE OF DISGUISES ...

What do you think?

Erm ... well ...

Better?

A little ...

AND BLUEBELL TRIED HIDING IN A SMALL, DARK SPACE ...

Are you OK, Bluebell?

Yes! I'm absolutely fine!

THAT NIGHT, WHILE EVERYONE ELSE SLEPT, JENNY LAY AWAKE ...

I'm frightened.

Maybe I shouldn't have encouraged the others to be detectives. I don't want them to be hurt!

Hey, is someone down there ...

... watching us?

THEY WOULD HAVE TO USE THE BACK DOOR TO THE ALLEY FROM NOW ON. SOMEONE WAS WATCHING THEIR EVERY MOVE ...

CHAPTER TEN

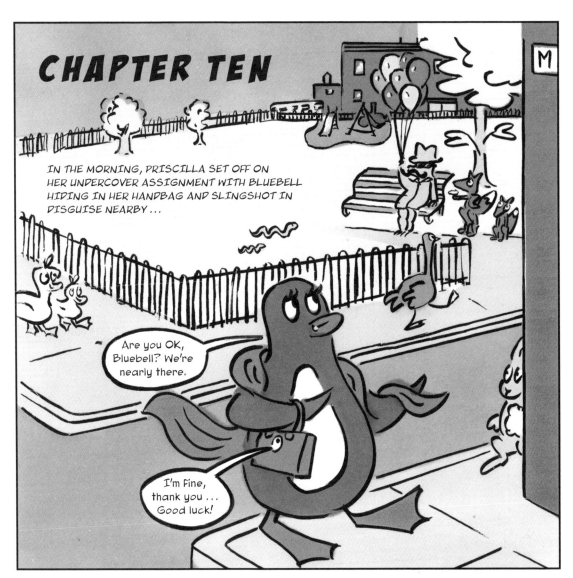

IN THE MORNING, PRISCILLA SET OFF ON HER UNDERCOVER ASSIGNMENT WITH BLUEBELL HIDING IN HER HANDBAG AND SLINGSHOT IN DISGUISE NEARBY...

Are you OK, Bluebell? We're nearly there.

I'm fine, thank you ... Good luck!

PRISCILLA ENTERED THE NEW YOU SALON ...

MANE ST

'New You' SALON

IMMEDIATELY, A POODLE WITH GIANT HAIR RACED FORWARD. IT WAS POOTLES LE FRIZZ ...

Dear poodle, you're so kind. I hope you can help with my hair disaster!

Dearest Madame, what is wrong?

Oh, *darling*, what with all the skiing vacations I've had this year ...

The ice! The snow! The roaring fires!

My perfect little feathers have split so horribly!

I shall never ski again!

WHUMPFH!

Madame has come to the right place. Just step through to the salon ...

Sniff ... sniff ...

THUNK!

She really is a GREAT actress!

Once we've worked our magic, your hair, your life, will be forever perfect!

Wow, this guy is so cheesy!

POOTLES LE FRIZZ LED PRISCILLA INSIDE THE SALON ...

Ah, here's my top stylist now!

Madame, I can't believe you're that age. You look at least three dog years younger!

So kind!

Sir will look radiant with his *color* enhancement!

Hi, I'm Penny! And I'll have you perfect as a poodle in no time!

Penny! *The* Penny? Dave Warthog's girlfriend?

Hey! I was thinking that, too!

Cut off her split ends, then give her the special conditioning treatment.

Sure, Pootles!

snip!

Darling girl, you're so pretty. Do you have a boyfriend? I've noticed some very handsome warthogs in this part of town!

Erm ... erm ... no. Erm ... I've decided to devote my life to hairdressing!

Oooh, she's very naughty. I can tell she's fibbing!

AS PENNY TRIMMED, PRISCILLA CONTINUED TO CHAT. BUT PENNY KEPT QUIET ...

I dated a boar once ... He was a real bore!

TIME FOR THE DRYER!

WHEN PRISCILLA AND THE OTHER CLIENTS WERE SITTING UNDER THE HAIR DRYERS, SPARKLY LIGHTS BEGAN TO FLICKER INSIDE. THEN THE ANIMALS STARTED TO TALK IN AN ODD, MECHANICAL WAY ...

HELLO. I AM CUDDLY, ADORABLE, AND COMPLETELY HOUSE-TRAINED.

Wh ... WHAT?

I DO NOT PASS WIND IN PUBLIC. I WOULD LOVE TO WALK ON A LEASH BY YOUR SIDE.

I DO NOT SWING ON EXPENSIVE FURNITURE OR MAKE FACES AT DINNER GUESTS. I WOULD MAKE A CHARMING COMPANION.

THE DRYERS LIFTED, AND BLUEBELL SAW THAT THERE WAS SOMETHING WRONG WITH PRISCILLA ...

AARGH! What should I do?!

THE PINK PERFECTOR POODLES PUSHED THE DAZED ANIMALS THROUGH A BACK DOOR ...

Get a move on, penguin!!

SORRY, SIR!

Pootles, the penguin's on to us!

Drat! Oooh! I think she's one of the new detectives ... Huh, she's quite a good actress! Well, she won't be troubling US for much longer!

I need Slingshot!

Quick, Slingshot! Follow that van!

MEANWHILE, BACK AT THE OFFICE, JENNY WAS OPENING THE MAIL. THE FIRST PACKAGE SMELLED, WELL, FUNNY ...

Roger! I think your mom's sent you a care package!

Oh boy!

How embarrassing!

CONTENTS: DUNG

JENNY OPENED AN ENVELOPE ...

GASP!

GIVE UP NOW OR U will DISAPPEAR 2!!

ROGER! Could I borrow your nose for a minute? We have been sent a threatening letter! Hmmm ... pink hairs stuck in the glue!

GIVE UP NOW OR U will DISAPPEAR 2!!

47

ROGER'S FINE GOURMET NOSE COULD DETECT ALL SORTS OF ODORS. HE SNIFFED THE ENVELOPE ...

Hmmmm ... tricky ... Hmmmm ... *tasty!* ...

I can smell lentils ...

some delicious spices ... in a tomato broth ...

IT HAS TO BE MULLIGATAWNY SOUP! Whoever licked this stamp had just eaten some. It's a popular Indian dish ...

Superb, Roger!

There are other scents on the letter ...

It smells of sawdust, metal cages, and dried food. I think this letter came from a store, one that sells ...

BEFORE HE COULD FINISH, BLUEBELL SCUTTLED IN ...

Pootles Le Frizz and the poodles aren't just hair washing, they're brain-washing, too! They've got Priscilla, and I think they're taking her to ...

A PET STORE!

Quick! Let's get the bike! We must rescue Priscilla and the others!

OK! Let me just get something first!

MEANWHILE, SLINGSHOT CHASED THE VAN AS IT SPED ALONG THE STREETS ...

PLF 3

THE VAN HAD TO STOP AT A CROSSING. NOW SLINGSHOT COULD USE HIS CELL PHONE ...

WALK

Tee-hee! That poodle guy's really annoyed. Let's cross back ... really S L O W L Y!

OK!

Jenny, I'm on the van! We're heading east along Mane Street.

BUT A GUST OF WIND TOOK THE PHONE AWAY!

Jenny here. We're on our way to the bike. Stay on the va ...

I've lost contact! How can I tell them where the van's going?

JENNY, ROGER, AND BLUEBELL LEAPT ON THE BIKE. JENNY PEDALED AS FAST AS SHE COULD AFTER SLINGSHOT ...

Mane Street, here we come!

THE 3·2·3

Ooops, sorry! Please charge your dry cleaning to us ... the 3-2-3 Detective Agency!

BUT WOULD THEY BE ABLE TO PICK UP THE VAN'S TRAIL? THEY ALL HOPED THAT SLINGSHOT HAD THOUGHT OF SOMETHING ...

CHAPTER ELEVEN

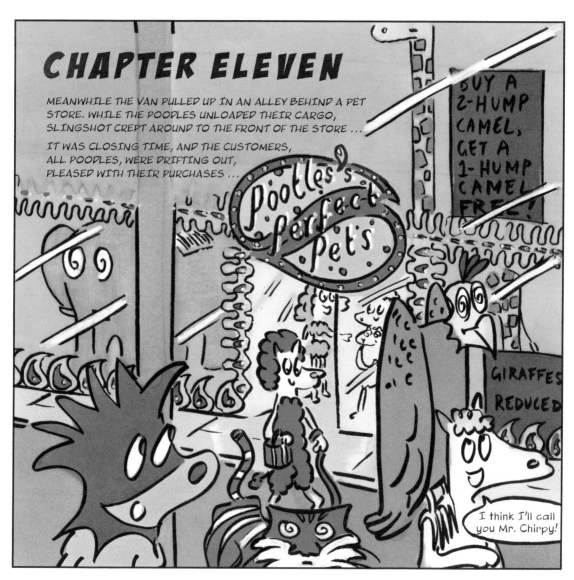

MEANWHILE THE VAN PULLED UP IN AN ALLEY BEHIND A PET STORE. WHILE THE POODLES UNLOADED THEIR CARGO, SLINGSHOT CREPT AROUND TO THE FRONT OF THE STORE...

IT WAS CLOSING TIME, AND THE CUSTOMERS, ALL POODLES, WERE DRIFTING OUT, PLEASED WITH THEIR PURCHASES...

Pootles's Perfect Pets

BUY A 2-HUMP CAMEL, GET A 1-HUMP CAMEL FREE!

GIRAFFES REDUCED

I think I'll call you Mr. Chirpy!

SUDDENLY, SLINGSHOT SAW A LADY POODLE CARRYING DIGBY'S MOM, ODORA! SHE HAD PUT A SPARKLY COAT ON HER. ODORA LOOKED OVERHEATED...

Odora isn't a pet! She has a home and a life, a family and friends! Pootles Le Frizz can't just steal her and sell her!

Do you like your new coat, Cuddles?

YES. THANK YOU SO MUCH.

A CUSTOMER SPOTTED SLINGSHOT ...

I want this funny bear-thing as well! It should fit ...

if we put the back seat down in the car!

Are you talking about me? WELL, I AM NOT FOR SALE, FUNNY DOG-THING!

We'll see about that!

INSIDE, POOTLES LE FRIZZ WAS COUNTING CASH FROM THE DAY'S TAKINGS ...

We want one of those funny-looking bear-things. You've got one outside. You know, they're always asleep, but this one is different. It's very lively ...

But it needs to be taught some manners!

We'll be back!

You want to buy THE SLOTH hiding outside? Give me a few days to tame him and he'll be in here with a price tag attached!

POOTLES LE FRIZZ GATHERED HIS WORKERS TOGETHER ...

So, Pink Perfectors! It seems the defectives of the 3-2-3 Agency have caught up with us. No, don't lock the door ...

Let's get this over with now! I'll get my new weapon ready!

OUTSIDE, SLINGSHOT WAS SHAKING WITH ANGER. HE WANTED TO GO IN AND SHOUT AT POOTLES LE FRIZZ ...

Hmmm ... but it's too dangerous to go in on my own! Now, what would Jenny do?

HE DECIDED TO WAIT FOR HIS FRIENDS.

51

CHAPTER TWELVE

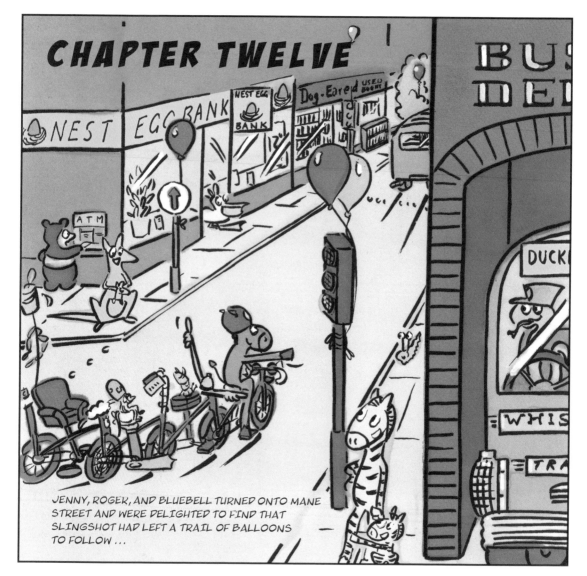

JENNY, ROGER, AND BLUEBELL TURNED ONTO MANE STREET AND WERE DELIGHTED TO FIND THAT SLINGSHOT HAD LEFT A TRAIL OF BALLOONS TO FOLLOW...

BUT JENNY FELT TIRED FROM ALL THE CYCLING...

SHE STOPPED...

Look, Roger! I'm more worried about rescuing Priscilla than having the picnic you packed. It's heavy, my legs hurt, and this is no time for cookies!

ROGER HOPPED FORWARD AND WHISPERED IN JENNY'S EAR ...

I'm sorry, Roger. It's a great idea to have a SECRET weapon. Let's go!

THEY FOLLOWED SLINGSHOT'S TRAIL TO A JUNCTION ...

They went thataway! Can I go home now?

NO TRESPASSING

Sure! Thanks!

THEY FOUND THEMSELVES AT THE ENTRANCE TO PRISTEENA, THE PRIVATE COMMUNITY FOR POODLES ...

PRISTEENA

POODLES' ENTRANCE ONLY
DELIVERIES/SERVANTS, ETC., ENTER VIA FROGSPAWN STREET

SECURITY

Well, I am NOT cycling another five miles! That is a very silly rule! Hmmpf! These poodles think they're better than everyone else!

FRANKIE'S COTTON CANDY

So, how do we get in?

TWO MINUTES LATER ...

Have you got enough now?

I think so!

CANDY

Good luck!

SORRY, WE ARE OUT OF COTTON CANDY!

Thanks, Frankie. OK, let's get the bike!

THE SECURITY GUARD WAS SLEEPING, SO ROGER GENTLY PUSHED THE BELL ON THE BIKE'S HANDLEBAR...

BELCH!!

Are you residents?

No, but we're looking to buy!

We thought we'd check out some of the neighborhoods here.

Yeah?

Yes. Actually, we're very fond of Indian food and would love to live near an Indian restaurant. Are there any in Pristeena?

Yeah, I think there's some in the Little India section ... or is it the Little Italy part?

I dunno. Here's a free map ...

Thanks!

THE GUARD PRESSED A BUTTON ...

ENTER

AND THE GATES TO PRISTEENA WERE OPENED ...

PRISTEENA

Oh, and don't belch in there. You'll be fined!

SECURITY

SECURITY

BELCH!!

Boy, sometimes I think this bike's alive! Anyway, well done, guys!

SOON THEY WERE GREETED BY A SERIES OF SIGNS ...

Welcome to

PRISTEENA
a Poodle Community

Visiting poodles: please wipe your feet before entering our special neighborhoods!

Is that really a doormat under the sign?

Looks like it!

TWO MINUTES LATER ...

ARE YOU REALLY SURE YOU WIPED YOUR FEET PROPERLY?

Really, really sure?

ANOTHER TWO MINUTES LATER ...

AND WHAT ABOUT YOUR HANDS?

FORGET IT!

THEY CAME TO THE FIRST NEIGHBORHOOD IN PRISTEENA, LITTLE ENGLAND ...

GAS $5.00

MINI MART

CASTLE APTS

YE OLDE MALL

NO HAWAIIAN SHIRTS

SAMURAI LUXURY APTS

24 HR MINI MART

CARP WASH

FLOSSING REQUIRED

CAR WASH $10-00

MINI MART

WHITE PALACE APTS

I'm Feeling a Little Hungary!

Perhaps you'd like a Little Turkey!

NO JOKING AROUND (SERIOUSLY)

PRETTY SOON THEY WERE IN LITTLE INDIA ... AND RACING TOWARD THEM WAS SLINGSHOT!

PINK PALACE

24 HR MINI MART

All the Raj

GAS $5-00

MAIL

NO LOUD GREETINGS

Hey, that's our bike! What have you done to my friends, you evil poodles?

It's us!

CRASH!

57

Hi, Slingshot!

Ooops!

THE FOUR STRUGGLED TO THEIR FEET. SLINGSHOT TOLD THEM WHAT HE'D SEEN ...

Look ... Odora Muskrat has been sold as a PET! And Priscilla is next!

And a couple wanted to buy me! Well, they can't have me, because I'm a detective, not a pet.

That's right, Slingshot. Well done! Now lead us back to the store!

JUST BEFORE THEY GOT THERE, THEY STOPPED OUTSIDE A RESTAURANT ...

All the Raj

ROGER WAS RIGHT ABOUT THE STAMP ON THE NASTY LETTER ...

All the Raj
FINE INDIAN CUISINE

MULLIGATAWNY SOUP
SAMOSA

SAG PANE
TIKKA MA

Well done, Roger!

Now we are about to arrest Pootles Le Frizz and his team. There are just four of us. We must ACT TOUGH!

Oh ... and we do have a secret weapon ... the cookie tin, Roger!

BUT JENNY WAS WORRIED. WHAT IF POOTLES LE FRIZZ HAD A SECRET WEAPON, TOO?

CHAPTER THIRTEEN

THE DETECTIVES EACH TOOK A DEEP BREATH AND STORMED INTO THE PET STORE. POOTLES LE FRIZZ BARELY BATTED AN EYELASH. HE REALLY WAS A COOL CUSTOMER, EVEN THOUGH HE WAS THE STOREKEEPER ...

SLINGSHOT RACED TOWARD PRISCILLA ...

PRISCILLA WAS IMMEDIATELY SURROUNDED BY THE PINK PERFECTOR POODLES ...

The secret weapon, Jenny! RELEASE THE DUNG!

SERVICE WITH A SMILE!

SMACK

DIRTY! DIRTY!

Well, I'm surprised by your determination, 3-2-3 defectives! I thought ransacking your office and sending the nasty letter would stop you! But it seems not ...

Look at you ... a hyperactive sloth ... a dung beetle with fancy food ideas ... a donkey with half a brain instead of none ... and the penguin here with split ends!

It's a shame your effort is WASTED!

Ooooooh ... how dare you! My friend Priscilla has lovely hair!

BLUEBELL WAS UPSET, TOO ...

Why hasn't he got anything nasty to say about me? Am I SO insignificant?

Did some THING say something?

Well, now the three of you are here, reunited with your penguin chum ...

THREE! He IS deliberately ignoring me!

You're so well camouflaged. We must use that to our advantage!

ANYWAY ... I must tell you my master plan before I ... ahem ... deal with you!

No, you don't have to tell us, really ...

The poodles of Pristeena are, thankfully, safely cocooned from the animal world and all its dirty, smelly imperfection! Yet some feel they'd be "happier" if they had a pet! They claim they're tired of knowing only poodles. Now, strange as that might sound ...

61

It's not strange! Pristeena's so boring! Who wants to spend their life with animals exactly the same as them? And that's not what that refrigerator magnate guy wanted!

Refrigerator magnet guy?

Well, it's true!

Whatever... Now, the only problem with letting you animals live here is... YOU ARE SOOOOO GROSS. You would BURP in our restaurants...

...PERSPIRE on our buses... PASS WIND in our library! YEUCH! I detest BODILY FUNCTIONS!

But NOW, with my brain-washing technique, you SAVAGES can become PROPER poodle-like pets! And I'll make a fortune!

Am I brilliant, or what?

OK, enough of this nonsense! Pootles Le Frizz, I am placing you under citizen's arrest!

Ha, you fools! I have a weapon, too! And mine's much bigger and better than yours!

Let me introduce you to my latest salon product! The world's STICKIEST mousse. Watch your eyes now!

HE AIMED AND FIRED... JENNY'S AND SLINGSHOT'S HAIR QUICKLY BECAME STICKY. IT HARDENED, AND THEY COULDN'T MOVE...

POOR ROGER HAD BEEN THROWN BACKWARD AND WAS STUCK TO THE WINDOW... BUT WHERE WAS BLUEBELL? HAD SHE GOTTEN AWAY?

CHAPTER FOURTEEN

POOTLES LE FRIZZ THREW JENNY AND SLINGSHOT INTO A SHOPPING CART...

Ha! Once they've had my brainwashing treatment, I'll put the donkey in the Bargain Bucket and sell the sloth as a large duster. Oooh! Or I could sell it to that silly couple!

THEN HE PEELED ROGER OFF THE WINDOW...

Not sure I'll be able to sell you, though.

I'll just stick a pin in you and send you to the Natural History Museum!

PHWAARGGH!

I suppose I'll have to clean up! Darn those cowardly Pink Perfector Poodles. Well, they're all FIRED!

I'm sorry, Roger. This mousse is just too sticky!

Hey! Is that the paper our ad's in?

So that's how Pootles knew about us! And it's why he doesn't know I exist! I'm almost impossible to see in that photograph. Oh dear, that seems like a long time ago!

THE B = 2 = 3 DETECTIVE AGENCY

Now, that's interesting. Does that mean there's a way to reverse the brainwashing?

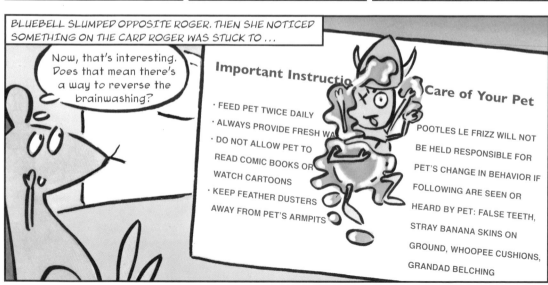

Important Instructio... **Care of Your Pet**

· FEED PET TWICE DAILY
· ALWAYS PROVIDE FRESH WA...
· DO NOT ALLOW PET TO READ COMIC BOOKS OR WATCH CARTOONS
· KEEP FEATHER DUSTERS AWAY FROM PET'S ARMPITS

POOTLES LE FRIZZ WILL NOT BE HELD RESPONSIBLE FOR PET'S CHANGE IN BEHAVIOR IF FOLLOWING ARE SEEN OR HEARD BY PET: FALSE TEETH, STRAY BANANA SKINS ON GROUND, WHOOPEE CUSHIONS, GRANDAD BELCHING

Hmmm! First I need to free Jenny, Slingshot, and Roger, so we can help the brainwashed animals ...

AS POOTLES LE FRIZZ HEADED TO THE BACK OF THE STORE, BLUEBELL TRIED TO THINK UP A PLAN TO SAVE HER FRIENDS ...

Now, what will unstick them from that horrible sticky mess?

I'm sick of poop. I need coffee!

THE COGS AND WHEELS IN HER MIND SPUN AS SHE GAZED FROM A SPRINKLER ON THE CEILING TO A NEARBY EXERCISE WHEEL ...

That's it! Cogs and wheels! I'm not strong enough to move the tap by paw, but there is a way I can turn it!

BLUEBELL FOUND SOME TWINE. SHE SCALED A PIPE TO THE CEILING ...

Come on, Bluebell. Forget you're scared of heights. You have to do this to save your friends!

SHE TIED THE TWINE TO THE SPRINKLER ON THE CEILING ...

THEN SHE LOOPED THE TWINE AROUND A TOWEL DISPENSER ... THEN A TRASH CAN ...

THEN FINALLY TIED IT TO THE EXERCISE WHEEL ...

I haven't played on one of these since kindergarten!

SHE STARTED TO RUN, JUST AS POOTLES MARCHED TO THE FRONT OF THE STORE ...

Dum-de-dum! Now, what next? Ah, brainwashing those meddlesome detectives!

65

CHAPTER FIFTEEN

SUDDENLY, TORRENTS OF WATER BEGAN TO RAIN DOWN! BLUEBELL'S PLAN FOR OPENING THE SPRINKLER HAD WORKED!

Aaaaaarrrrrr-rrrrrrrrggggggg-gggggghhhhh!!

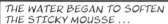

THE WATER BEGAN TO SOFTEN THE STICKY MOUSSE ...

POOTLES WAS FURIOUS. HE TRIED TO SHINNY UP THE PIPE TO TURN OFF THE TAP ...

Stop it! Stop it!

BUT THE FLOOD OF WATER KEPT THROWING HIM BACK ...

Oh, my curly perm!

MEANWHILE, JENNY, SLINGSHOT, AND ROGER COULD WIGGLE THEIR HOOVES, TOES, OR FEELERS AGAIN ...

WHEN THE SPRINKLER SYSTEM FINALLY CUT OFF, SLINGSHOT TACKLED POOTLES ...

Don't even think of speaking!

I can take it from here, Slingshot!

Pootles Le Frizz, you have been very, very naughty! I am placing you under citizen's arrest!

And I'm going to tell your mom, too!

Whatever. But I still beat you defectives! I'll never tell you how to reverse the brainwashing done to your split-ended pal! ... And anyway, who on earth are you?

I AM BLUEBELL, and I know how to reverse your treatment! Slingshot, can you guard him? Jenny, Roger, and I have some entertaining to do!

RATS!

BLUEBELL BECKONED ROGER AND JENNY TO GO OUTSIDE WITH HER ...

THEN THEY LEAPT ON THEIR BIKE. BUT INSTEAD OF LEAVING, THEY PEDALED BACK INTO THE STORE ...

Tonight, for your delight, we present the 3-2-3 Clown Company! Enjoy!

WHEELIE!

Stop! Don't make them laugh!

Ahh, is someone feeling left out?

BEANZ

Dinner is served!

BEANZ

Could I have extra sausages with mine?

Delicious!

TURTLES

Who's a clever bike, then? Yes, you are!

AH-A

TICKLE
TICKLE

YIKES!

AH-AH

AH-AH-AH

THE ANIMALS WERE FREE AGAIN ...

Ho-ho!

Oh, do it again! Do it again!

Hee-hee, my sides hurt!

SQUEAK

SQUEAL

SQUEAK

Mine, too!

Could someone help me up?

LAUGHTER WAS THE CURE FOR POOTLES'S PERFECTING SPELL ...

Ha-ha-ha! ... Where am I?

Now, this may sting a little!

Seriously, guys, could someone help me up?

Five bucks? That Le Frizz guy's got a lot of nerve!

AND PRISCILLA ...

PRISCILLA!

?

PRISCILLA!

WAS HAPPY TO SEE ...

HER FELLOW DETECTIVES ...

Erm, darlings ... why am I covered in poop?

EPILOGUE

THE 3-2-3 DETECTIVES WERE THE TOAST OF WHISKA CITY. BACK AT NUMBER 8 PLATYPUS PLACE, THEY BASKED IN THE PRAISE...

AND THEY ALL DANCED UNTIL THEIR PAWS OR HOOVES OR LEGS OR FLIPPERS FELT VERY TIRED INDEED . . .

THE END

For Gabriel Groundhog, with love

Acknowledgments: Thank you to everyone at Amulet Books for their considerable and MUCH appreciated help in creating this story, especially Susan Van Metre, Chad W. Beckerman, Amalia Ellison, and Scott Auerbach. I'd also like to thank Barbara Markowitz for her tremendous support.
Love to Josh, always.
And look, Mum, it finally got done!

Artist's note:
The pictures in this book were created with marker pens.

Library of Congress Cataloging-in-Publication Data

Robinson, Fiona, 1965–
The 3-2-3 Detective Agency : the disappearance of Dave Warthog /
by Fiona Robinson.
p. cm.
Summary: Five animal friends decide to form a detective agency in Whiska City, where they investigate the rash of disappearances linked to a poodle beauty salon.
Hardcover ISBN 978-0-8109-8489-9 (Harry N. Abrams)
Paperback ISBN 978-0-8109-7094-6 (Harry N. Abrams)
[1. Graphic novels. 2. Mystery and detective stories. 3. Animals—Fiction.]
I. Title. II. Title: 3-2-3 Detective Agency. III. Title: Disappearance of Dave Warthog. IV. Title: Three-two-three Detective Agency in The disappearance of Dave Warthog.

PZ7.7.R633Aaf 2009
[E]—dc22
2008037171

Printed and bound in China
10 9 8 7 6 5 4 3 2 1

Amulet Books are available at special discounts when purchased in quantity for premiums and promotions as well as fundraising or educational use. Special editions can also be created to specification. For details, contact specialmarkets@abramsbooks.com or the address below.

THE ART OF BOOKS SINCE 1949
115 West 18th Street
New York, NY 10011
www.abramsbooks.com